LIFE IN THE FAST LANE

INSIDE A FORMULA 1 CAR

COLLIN MACARTHUR

Cavendish Square
New York

Published in 2015 by Cavendish Square Publishing, LLC
243 5th Avenue, Suite 136, New York, NY 10016

First Edition

CPSIA Compliance Information: Batch #WS14CSQ

Library of Congress Cataloging-in-Publication Data
MacArthur, Collin, author.
Inside a Formula 1 car / Collin MacArthur.
pages cm. — (Life in the fast lane)
Includes bibliographical references and index.
ISBN 978-1-62713-034-9 (hardcover) ISBN 978-1-62713-036-3 (ebook)
1. Formula One automobiles—Juvenile literature. 2. Automobile racing—Juvenile literature. 3. Grand Prix racing—Juvenile literature. I. Title. II. Title: Inside a Formula One car.

TL236.265.M33 2015
629.228—dc23

2014010507

Editorial Director: Dean Miller
Art Director: Jeffrey Talbot
Production Manager: Jennifer Ryder-Talbot
Production Editor: David McNamara

Packaged for Cavendish Square Publishing, LLC by BlueApple*Works* Inc.
Managing Editor: Melissa McClellan
Designer: Tibor Choleva
Photo Research: Joshua Avramson
Copy Editor: Kira Freed

The photographs in this book are used by permission and through the courtesy of:
Cover photo, peepo/Vetta/Getty Images; p. 4 © efecreata media group/Shutterstock.com; p. 6, 9 © Everett Collection/Shutterstock.com; p. 10–11, 12 © Natursports/Shutterstock.com; p. 14–15, 18 © emran/Shutterstock.com; p. 17 © Pierre Jean Durieu/Dreamstime.com; p. 21, 29 © Ahmad Faizal Yahya/Shutterstock.com; p. 22 © Julie Lucht/Shutterstock.com; p. 25 © Jaggat Rashidi/Shutterstock.com; p. 26 © Mikhail Kolesnikov/Shutterstock.com; p. 30–31 © Tatiana Popova/Shutterstock.com; p. 32 © Serjio74/Shutterstock.com; p 34, 36–37 © Chen WS/Shutterstock.com; p. 39 © cjmac /Shutterstock.com

Printed in the United States of America

CONTENTS

Formula 1 cars have very powerful engines.

INTRODUCTION

The driver quickly glances up from the track. A race official is waving a colored flag. As the driver zooms by, he sees a blur of bright yellow. Another racer has spun off the track. How many others are left in the race? Twelve? Eleven? No time to count. Here comes a sharp corner. Watch out! The driver makes a split-second decision. Hit the brake. Ease up. Steer left—but not too sharply! Made it. That was close!

Formula 1 cars are among the fastest and most powerful on the planet, and the world of Formula 1 racing is tense and sometimes scary. The cars move so fast that one-hundredth of a second can put a driver in first place! This book takes you inside this world—with its big races, brave drivers, and swift pit crews. Of course, you'll also read about the amazing machines themselves. So buckle up and put both hands on the wheel. Start your engines!

People have always liked watching car races.

1 SPEED APPEAL

Back in the early twentieth century, cars were a brand new way to get where you needed to go. Early cars were slow and fragile—small buggies perched on bicycle wheels and powered by small, noisy engines. It wasn't long before the desire for speedier cars took hold. Some people spent a lot of money to make their cars go fast. They wanted to prove to the public that their cars were faster than all others. Auto racing had begun.

The idea of racing for money or trophies is not new. Humans have raced one another on foot or horseback, in boats, or at track meets for thousands of years. Racing is a popular form of entertainment. It gives people a chance to show off their talents.

As cars improved, the best drivers challenged one another to **competitions**. They wanted to settle once and for all which automobile was fastest.

Races were held anywhere an audience could be found, even at county fairs. There were few rules, and those that did exist often were broken. Some drivers even cheated during competitions. Early races could be unsafe. The audience had little protection from the cars. Being too near a speeding car could lead to serious injuries! Still, people came from miles around to watch racing events.

Formula 1 Is Born

The United States wasn't the only country caught up in racing fever. Europeans were also discovering the thrill. Racing cars were much different then. Their tires were thinner and had spokes, like bicycle wheels. Engines were heavier and were placed in the front of cars. Races were different, too. In 1895, there were no racetracks. Races were held right in the middle of cities. To be a **spectator**, all you had to do was look out your window!

The first race took place on the streets of France. The event was called the Grand Prix, which means "grand prize" in French. Grand Prix racing is another name for

Early racing cars were rather slow compared to the vehicles of present-day Formula 1 competitions.

Formula 1 racing. In that first Grand Prix race, the winner's car drove about 70 mph (112.7 km/h). Today's cars can reach speeds three times that fast!

Thanks to the Grand Prix, racing became more popular than ever. People wanted to know which country could produce the fastest car and the best driver. They wanted to crown a world champion. But the safety and rules of motor racing were shaky. In 1950, a group called the Federation International de l'Automobile (FIA) was formed. Its mission was to oversee the sport of auto

Every design detail of modern Formula 1 race cars is controled by FIA.

racing. Under FIA leadership, the Formula 1 World Championship began in 1950.

To make things consistent and fair, the FIA set guidelines for Formula 1 cars, including length, weight, and engine type. (Together, these guidelines make up the "formula" for which Formula 1 is named.) FIA also created rules to make races safer for the competitors and the fans. The group improved racecar speed and tire design. The FIA still **governs** motor racing today and continues to make the sport stronger by changing the "formula" and improving other guidelines.

Formula 1 drivers reach record-breaking speeds.

2 FAST AND FURIOUS

Through the years, Formula 1 cars continue to get faster and more exciting. A car today can reach 100 mph (161 km/h) in less than four seconds. A Formula 1 car speeding down the **straightaway**—a long, straight stretch of track—of a racing **circuit** can reach 232 mph (373 km/h). Ignoring turns for a moment, a baseball player running that fast could circle the bases in just over one second!

Many improvements have been made to reach these record-breaking speeds. Circuits are safer. Drivers are better trained. Pit crews are faster and smarter. They study the racetracks. They test each piece of equipment carefully. They spend long nights preparing for races. We'll consider all of these issues later. For now, let's focus on the cars.

Full Speed Ahead

As races became more popular, Formula 1 designers realized that the less cars weighed, the faster they could go. Imagine having to move around while carrying a backpack full of books. The extra weight of the books would create resistance, or **drag**, and slow you down. In racing, drag slows cars down and weakens their performance.

It became important to build lighter and lighter cars. The **chassis**, or frame, of an old Formula 1 car was made from heavy sheet metal. Over time, the heavy metals were replaced with lighter materials—aluminum at first, and these days carbon fiber.

Formula 1 racing cars have their powerful engines mounted in the rear.

The engine was moved from the front to the rear of the car. This change eliminated the need for a long drive shaft. A drive shaft helps get the engine's power to the rear tires. With the new design, the engine was already right beside the rear tires.

Formula 1 cars also got faster by being built lower to the ground. Older cars were shaped like cigars. But new technology made the cars flatter. Today, they are so low to the ground that the drivers sit in a reclining position when they drive. Sometimes they have trouble seeing over the steering wheel!

Just as the chassis was made out of a lighter material, so were the new engines, which had a lot more power. For a time, they also had more cylinders. Cylinders are the chambers through which the fuel passes. The more cylinders an engine has, the more fuel there is to power the car. Regular cars usually have four or six cylinders. A Formula 1 engine used to have ten or twelve, but later "formulas" dropped that number to eight and then six. To make up for lost power, newer designs harness energy from braking and **exhaust** gases that would otherwise escape as heat.

Keeping a Firm Grip

Formula 1 cars soon became too light. They began losing their grip on the track. Vehicles kept spinning off the circuit. Speeds were faster than ever, but drivers were in too much danger.

Designers turned to gravity for help. The minimum weight of a Formula 1 car—with its driver but not fuel—was raised and is now at 1,523 pounds (691 kg). That's still very light. Regular cars can weigh nearly three times as much. Designers also spent

Early Formula 1 racing cars looked nothing like the F1 racing cars look today.

A member of a Formula 1 technical crew prepares slick tires for a race in dry weather conditions.

a lot of time improving tires. Cars need excellent tires to get a good grip on the track. A Formula 1 driver gets fifteen sets of tires for each race. Three sets of tires are "wet" tires, used only when it rains. These wet tires contain grooves that help push away rain to prevent slipping. The tires that are used in dry weather are called slicks. They are completely bald! They look as though their treads have completely worn off. Because the tires are smooth, more of the tire rubber can touch the track at all times. As a result, the tires gain the maximum grip, or **traction**, on the track. Grip is very important for both speed and safety. Before every race, Formula 1 tires are wrapped in heated blankets. The heat helps improve their traction during the race.

Sprouting Wings

Aerodynamics measures how air affects an object's movement. If a car is not aerodynamic, wind cannot flow smoothly over it. Instead, the wind creates drag, which slows down the car. Designers discovered how important **downforce** was to a Formula 1 car's speed. Downforce pushes the tires onto the track and increases their grip, which helps the car handle turns better. To produce more downforce, designers put special wings on the cars. Like aircraft wings, they cause air to flow at different speeds over the top and bottom. Since they're upside down, the difference in pressure helps the car stay on the ground instead of taking to the skies.

A Formula 1 car has two wings—one in the back and the other near the nose. Both can be adjusted to produce extra downforce. Too little downforce will prevent the tires from gripping the track well and make it easier for the driver to lose control of the car. Too much downforce may keep the car from steering well.

HIT THE BRAKES

Formula 1 cars fly around the circuit just inches apart. They also must be able to stop on a dime. Just how quickly can they stop? An F1 car going about 60 mph (100 km/h) can stop in about 49 feet (15 m) —less than one-third the stopping distance of an average road car.

These technicians are getting ready to install and adjust the Formula 1 car's front wings.

A Formula 1 driver concentrating for his race.

3 READY FOR ACTION

Formula 1 drivers do so much more than just sit down on the job. Being an F1 driver requires almost superhuman fitness. As drivers **accelerate**, they feel a force pushing them back into their seat. When they change direction, the same force pushes them to the side. This force, called g-force (G), is the force of gravity acting on a body during fast changes in speed or direction. (You've probably felt it on a roller coaster.) During a race, Formula 1 drivers can be exposed to more than four Gs—four times the force of Earth's gravity! It takes great strength and endurance to go over 200 mph (322 km/h) for ninety minutes or more and make split-second decisions with that much force acting on them.

To boost their fitness, drivers train by doing intensive running, swimming, or other **cardiovascular** exercise. They also strengthen their neck and arm muscles with special equipment. Before a race, drivers eat foods rich in **carbohydrates** to have energy and stamina for the race. They also drink a lot of water to make sure they don't become **dehydrated** from sweating. Temperatures in the seat, or **cockpit**, can soar to 122° F (50° C), and drivers may lose up to seven pounds (3 kg) of sweat during a race.

In The Driver's Seat

Grand Prix cars must be light, low, and compact, so Formula 1 drivers need to put up with a snug fit. In fact, the cockpit of each car is specially molded to fit the shape of its driver! Drivers wear special seat belts that lock at five different points. In a crash, a driver pushes a center button to release the harness. The steering wheel is also removable. The "formula" requires the driver to be able to get out within five seconds.

Formula 1 drivers wear four layers of fire-resistant clothes, including socks, gloves, and long underwear. These clothes keep drivers safe in blazes up to 1,300° F (704.4° C). In addition, drivers wear protective helmets. The helmets are very strong. A stone traveling at 300 mph (483 km/h) could hit them and not even crack the outside.

Drivers have to excercise a lot to stay in shape.

Formula 1 drivers do not have much room to move around in the cockpit.

A newer safety feature is a special collar called the Head and Neck Support (HANS) system. Required since 2003, it protects a driver's head and neck if the car slows down quickly as a result of an accident.

Hot Wheel

The tiny cockpit space has a lot of gadgets that help the Formula 1 cars go at top speed. Drivers don't have any focus to spare during a race. They can't be fussing with tricky controls or hunting for hidden gauges.

FORMULA 1 FLOPS

New Formula 1 cars have come out over the years, but not all of them have been improvements. One team built a car with six wheels—two normal ones in back and four very small ones in front—hoping this would improve the car's grip and aerodynamics. The small tires wore down too quickly. One of the first drivers to use wings put them on stilts on the back of the car. During the race, one wing collapsed from the speed and the wind. Still, it pays to try new things.

So over time, almost all the controls have moved onto the steering wheel. Two levers let drivers switch gears with simple flicks of the wrist. Buttons warn the driver of problems with oil pressure or engine overheating. Drivers speak with their pit crews through radio contact. Drivers can read their cars' speed and can see how long it took to drive a lap. Some cockpit buttons are top secret to help teams keep their competitive edge. All these buttons and displays give drivers information and let them concentrate on sharp turns and high speeds. It's like having an invisible copilot.

Gearing Up For The Race

The days leading up to Sunday's race are almost as tense as the race itself. Thursday is inspection time. Trained FIA officials, called **scrutineers**, inspect each Formula 1 car. Scrutineers have a checklist of dozens of items. They check to see if anything is missing, loose, or poorly constructed. Their job is to make sure each car meets all technical and safety guidelines. A car can be disqualified if just one item is not perfect. Later in the weekend, scrutineers will recheck any car

Scrutineers and crew technicians work together to make sure that cars are in perfect shape for the race.

involved in an accident or changed by its team. Cars are also weighed to be sure they meet the minimum weight requirement.

On Friday and Saturday, drivers learn the circuit and test their cars during practice laps. They may practice up to three hours on Friday and one hour on Saturday. Their other hours are filled with meetings. The teams discuss strategies and possible technical problems. These meetings are the last chance to work out problems and decide on the best settings for the track. Racers test their steering on sharp turns. Wings

Drivers checking the circuit before the race.

may need fixing to produce more downforce. Tires may need adjustments. On practice days, the racetrack becomes a laboratory.

Saturday afternoon is the time to qualify. During a one-hour session, drivers speed around the track to prove they're fast enough to compete. All the cars reach incredible speeds, but only the best drivers qualify. The driver who records the fastest lap time is awarded the "pole position." This car gets a slight head start in the race and will have the best approach to the first

All is quiet and peaceful at a track before the race begins.

corner. Because split seconds count in Formula 1 races, everyone wants the advantage of the pole position.

On Sunday morning, it is tradition to have a drivers' parade. They are driven around the track, sometimes individually in an open top car and sometimes collectively on the back of a truck. Aside from that, they try to relax and get ready for the race, which will start soon.

WOMEN TRAILBLAZERS

In 1909, Alice Ramsey made the shocking announcement that she would drive from New York City to Los Angeles. Big deal? At that time, it was. Men thought women couldn't handle driving. Ramsey made the journey safely, and today women drive everywhere. That includes Formula 1 racing. In 1958, Maria Teresa de Filippis became the first woman to race in Formula 1. In 1980, Desire Wilson became the first—and only—woman to win a Formula 1 race, at Brands Hatch in England. Simona de Silvestro, a young driver, would like to change that. She is training to compete in Formula 1 races in 2015.

Racing cars line up on the starting grid moments before the Formula 1 races start.

4 RACE AGAINST TIME

The start of a Grand Prix race is thrilling. It's also one of the best times during the race to get ahead. Finally the race is underway, but the cars aren't going that fast. Is there a problem?

Not at all. Just before the official start, race cars go through a final practice. Drivers' teams move their cars into position at the front of the track. This area is called the starting grid. The cars line up in order of how they qualified. The pole position car is in front. The next-fastest car is second, and so on. Drivers circle the track one last time to warm up. This is called the formation lap. Competitors weave their vehicles left and right, warming the tires to get better traction. The cars drive the formation lap at about 110 mph (177 km/h). At last, all eyes look up at a lighting fixture overhead. Five red lights turn on one second apart. When the last one goes out, the race has begun!

Ahead of the Pack

Just staying on the racetrack is hard enough, but Formula 1 drivers have to put in more effort if they want to either take the lead or maintain it. The best drivers are not just fast—they're smart!

Drivers use different strategies to overtake other vehicles. One of the more famous techniques is called slipstreaming. A driver sneaks up behind the car directly ahead of him. The lead car has to battle high winds. The car behind the lead car is less affected by these winds and has better aerodynamics. Just at the right moment on

a straightaway, the second car slips to the side of the lead car and pulls ahead. Meanwhile, the lead car continues to battle the wind and falls behind.

In the Pit

One of the most exciting times in a Grand Prix race occurs when the cars aren't moving. These are pit stops. Now the focus switches from the speed of the cars to the speed of the mechanics. The "lollipop man" holds up a sign so a driver can easily find the right pit stall. The car exits the circuit and comes to a screeching halt.

Drivers jockey for position to win the race.

A team of mechanics is already in position. Having fast hands is very important. It's up to the pit crew to fix the problems—in a matter of seconds!

Every crew member is aware of where to go and what to do. That's because they are in constant radio communication with the driver. They already know if the car is having problems. Crew members break down big tasks into smaller ones. To change a tire, two "jack men" use a special device to lift the car. Two tire carriers replace the old tire with a new one. Then the tire changer fastens the new tire with a high-speed airgun.

It can get crowded and tense in the pit, but safety comes first. If pit crew members aren't careful, they could burn themselves on the car's hot chassis. One crew member stands ready to put out any fires. Pit stops are safer than they used to be because no refueling is allowed. Drivers must start with enough fuel to finish the race.

"DNF" (Did Not Finish)

Fewer than half of the Formula 1 vehicles in each race cross the finish line. Some cars collide during tight turns. Some spin off the

Pit crew members must move as fast as possible when servicing their driver's race car.

track. Others have electrical problems or tires that get punctured by loose objects. When an accident occurs, a vehicle that looks like a police car enters the track. This is the **pace car**. When drivers see the pace car, they must slow down. They drive behind it until race officials are sure that the damaged car has been cleared from the track.

Sweet Victory!

Using one last blast of speed, one car crosses the finish line first. The checkered flag whips around in all directions. Winning at Formula 1 takes a delicate mix of skill, determination, and luck. The top ten drivers who finish score points. Twenty-five points go to the winner, eighteen points for second place, fifteen for third place, then ten, eight, six, four, two, and down to one point for tenth place. After a full year of competing, the driver with the most points is named world champion.

A driver who finishes tenth is happy to accept his one point. He hopes he can finish stronger next time. Meanwhile, the first-place winner can't celebrate for long. He will have to work even harder next time.

Looking Toward The Future

Along with more great races, what's next for Formula 1? As the world changes, it's more important than ever to think about the environment. Car racing relies on fuels that won't last forever, and burning them causes pollution. In recent years, improving F1 performance with fewer resources has become an important focus. Formula 1's brightest minds are coming up with new technologies to help both open-wheel racing and the entire car industry survive. As a result, Formula 1 drivers will continue to get even more performance out of their cars.

DRIVER'S ED

Would you like to be a Formula 1 driver? Many of today's F1 superstars got their start in school. There are many racing schools in the world. Students begin by driving sedans. They take instruction from professional race car drivers who sit beside them. Students work their way up to racing single-seaters that are similar to Formula 1 cars. Some schools even send their top students to all-expenses-paid races.

WORDS TO KNOW

accelerate: to speed up

aerodynamics: the science of how wind and air propel or slow down a moving object

carbohydrates: nutrients found in foods such as bread, pasta, and potatoes that provide the body with energy

cardiovascular: related to the heart and blood vessels

chassis: the frame of a Formula 1 racing vehicle

circuits: racing tracks

cockpit: the space where a Formula 1 driver sits

competitions: events or tests of skill between two or more people

dehydrated: having lost a large amount of water from the body

drag: a force that slows down motion

WORDS TO KNOW

downforce: an aerodynamic force that pushes the tires of a Formula 1 car down to the racetrack

exhaust: the mix of gases that an engine produces

governs: makes laws or rules for a group of people

pace car: a car that limits how fast other cars can go during a race if an accident happens or something is blocking the track

scrutineers: officials who inspect Formula 1 cars before a race

spectator: a person who watches a sporting event for enjoyment

straightaways: long stretches of racetrack without any curves

traction: the amount of grip that tires have on the track or road

FURTHER READING

Books

Being a Formula One Driver
Adam Sutherland
Minneapolis, MN
Lerner Publications
2012

Formula One
Adrianna Morganelli
New York, NY
Crabtree Publishing Company
2006

Formula 1
Tyrone Georgiou
New York, NY
Gareth Stevens Publishing
2011

Websites

Formula 1

www.formula1.com

This is the official Website of Formula 1 racing. It contains sections on understanding F1 racing and on rules and regulations.

F1forKidz

f1forkidz.com

This Formula 1 site, which is geared toward young people, includes sections on schedules, teams and drivers, results, and photos.

IndyCar Series

www.indycar.com

This is the official Website of the Indy Racing League, which sponsors open-wheel auto racing in the United States. The site includes current news, schedules, race results, and statistics. It also offers information about the cars, drivers, teams, gear, and racing procedures.

Organizations

The Grand Prix Drivers' Association (GPDA)

Monaco
The GPDA represents racing car drivers in areas such as safety, rule changes, insurance polices, and even the image of F1 drivers.

International Automobile Federation (FIA)

Paris, France
Phone: +33 1 4312 44 55
www.fia.com
FIA governs the sport of F1 racing. It creates the rules and regulations under which the series competes.

INDEX

Page numbers in purple are images.

INDEX

About the Author

Collin MacArthur is a former automotive engineer with a master's degree in mechanical engineering. Today, Collin works as a freelance automotive interest writer. He lives in Florida with his wife, son, and dog.